¡El día del bebé!

Baby Day!

¡El día del bebé!

Baby Day!

Escrito e ilustrado por **Nancy Elizabeth Wallace**

Traducido por **Annie García Kaplan Ed. D.**

Houghton Mifflin Company Boston 2003

All rights reserved. For information about permission to reproduce
selections from this book, write to Permissions, Houghton Mifflin
Company, 215 Park Avenue South, New York, New York 10003.

www.houghtonmifflinbooks.com

The text of this book is set in 18-point Goudy.
The illustrations were created using origami and found
paper, Scherenschnitte scissors, a glue stick, tape, and tweezers.

Library of Congress Cataloging-in-Publication Data
Wallace, Nancy Elizabeth.
Baby day! / written and illustrated by Nancy Elizabeth Wallace.
p. cm.
Summary: Baby eats, takes a bath, gets dressed,
plays, takes a nap, and then gets busy again.
ENG ISBN 0-618-27576-2   SP ISBN 0-618-38795-1
[1. Babies—Fiction. 2. Stories in rhyme.] I. Title.
PZ8.3.W1585 Bab 2003   [E]—dc21   2002005087

Printed in Singapore
TWP 10 9 8 7 6 5 4 3 2 1

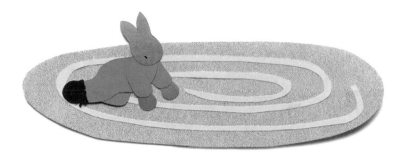

pijamas

PJs

¡El día del bebé! ¡Levántate, levántate! ¿Qué vamos a hacer?

Baby day! Up! Up! Up!

cuchara
spoon

babero
bib

Super Baby!

vaso
cup

plato bowl

Te daré de comer en tu vaso y plato.

Eat good food, bowl and cup.

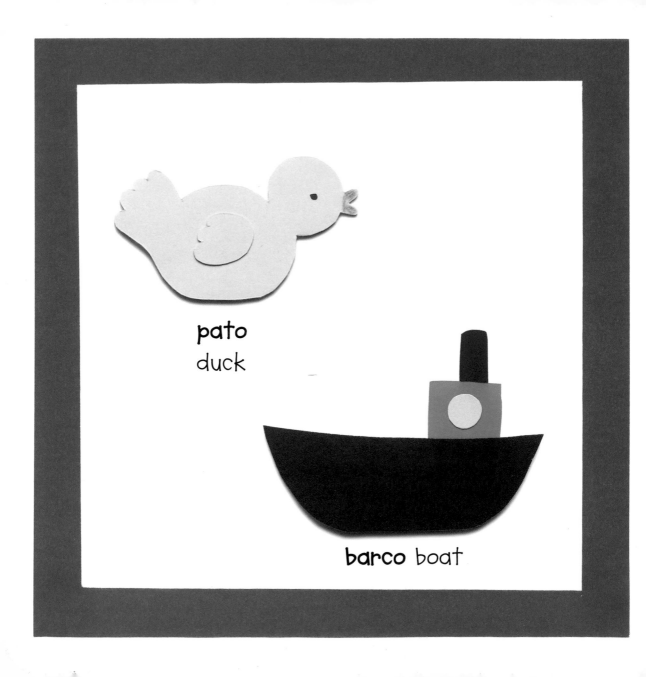

pato
duck

barco boat

Te bañaré junto a tu barco y pato.

Take a bath, in a tub, scrub a dub, scrub a dub, gently rub.

móvil
mobile

abeja
bee

mariposa
butterfly

mariquita
ladybug

Te haré cosquillas en tu
estómago, pies, nariz y mejillas.

Touch your tummy. Wiggle your toes.
Kiss your cheek. Nuzzle your nose.

calcetines
socks

mameluco
playsuit

botas booties

Te prepararé
y te vestiré.

Get all dressed,
shoes and socks.

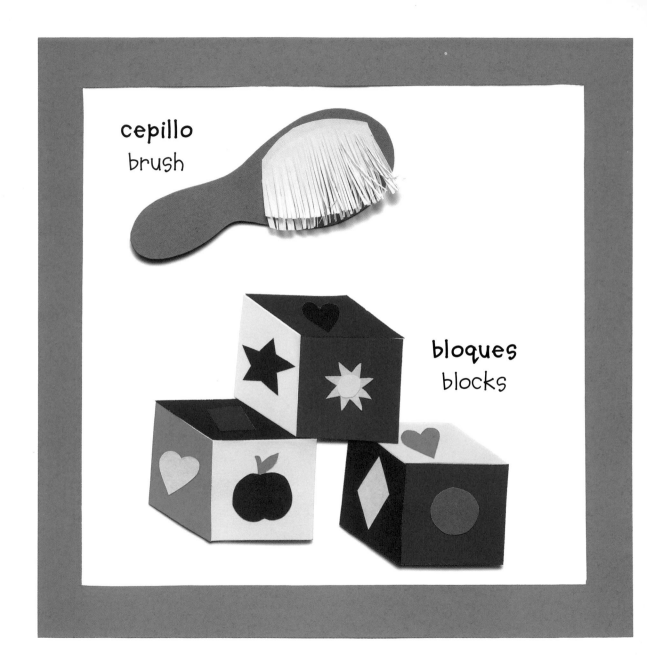

cepillo
brush

bloques
blocks

Y mientras juegas con tus bloques, tu pelo cepillaré.

Brush your hair.
Play with blocks.

carro
car

bola
ball

blue — azul
green — verde
yellow — amarillo
orange — anaranjado
red — rojo

pila de aros
stacking rings

Vamos a empujar, arrastrar, rodar y amontonar.

Push and pull.
Roll and stack.

arca de juguetes

toy box

Gatearás y explorarás para alante y para atrás.

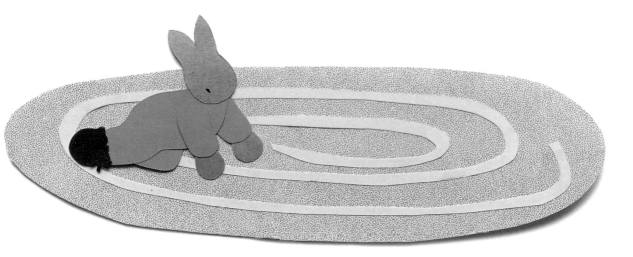

Baby go! Baby go! Baby come back!

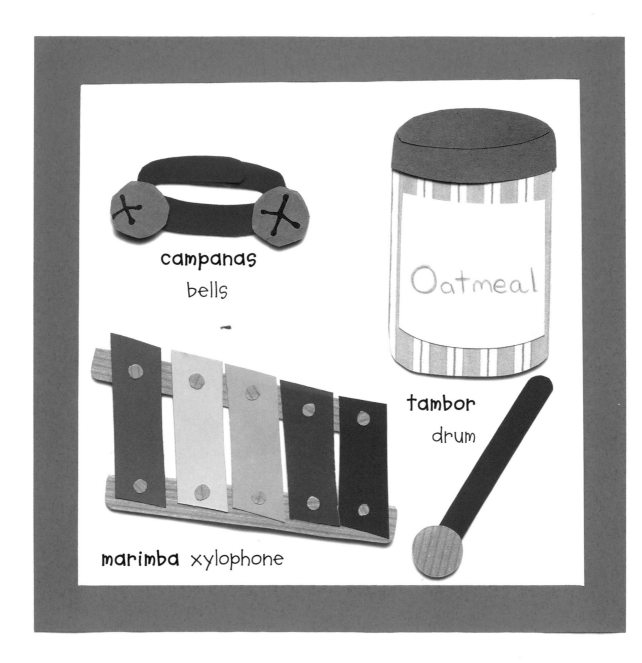

campanas

bells

Oatmeal

tambor

drum

marimba xylophone

Cantaremos y aplaudiremos.

Clap and sing.

librero bookcase

Un libro leeremos.

Read a book.

hoja
leaf

flor
flower

grama grass

Iremos a pasear,
saludar y mirar.

Go outside. Look, look, look.

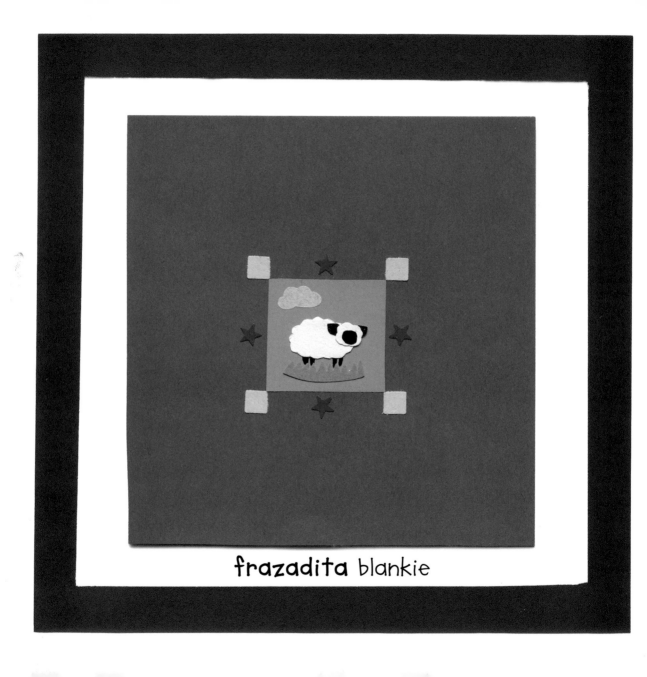

frazadita *blankie*

Dormirás una siesta
y descansarás…

Take a nap, rest, and then . . .

oso
bear

…despertarás y te preguntaré:
"¿Qué vamos a hacer durante el día del bebé?"

Up, sweet baby! Busy again.

acaricia cuddle • sonríe smile • canta sing • ríe laugh • habla talk • juega play • lee read